imaginative

bitty ⭐ baby

loves the snow

by Kirby Larson
& Sue Cornelison

⭐ American Girl®

Special thanks to Dr. Laurie Zelinger, consultant,
child psychologist, and registered play therapist.
Dr. Zelinger reviewed and helped shape the "For Parents"
section, which was written by editorial staff.

Published by American Girl Publishing
Copyright © 2013 American Girl

Questions or comments? Call 1-800-845-0005,
visit **americangirl.com,** or write to Customer Service,
American Girl, 8400 Fairway Place, Middleton, WI 53562-0497.

Printed in China
13 14 15 16 17 18 19 20 LEO 10 9 8 7 6 5 4 3 2 1

All American Girl and Bitty Baby marks are trademarks of American Girl.

Series Editorial Development: Jennifer Hirsch & Elizabeth Ansfield
Art Direction and Design: Gretchen Becker
Production: Tami Kepler, Judith Lary, Paula Moon, Kristi Tabrizi

For Louise
K.L.

To Sam with love
S.C.

Bitty Baby and I opened the curtains.

"It's all white outside," said Bitty Baby.

"Snow!" I said. "Let's go play."

"Dress up nice and warm, like me," said Daddy.
"It's cold out there. *Brrr.*"

Bitty Baby and I pulled on warm sweaters and tights
and snowsuits and hats.

"We're ready," I said. "We're going to build the best
snowman ever."

My brother pulled Bitty Baby and me in the
sled, past Daddy shoveling the driveway, to
the hill by our house.

"Yay!" Bitty Baby and I tumbled off.
"This is the perfect snow for building."

"And it's the perfect
snow for sledding
with my friends,"
said my brother.
He hurried to the
sledding hill.

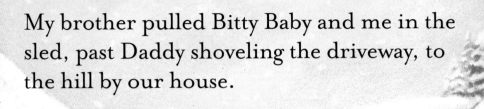

"Let's start our snowman," I said. Bitty Baby and I scooped up some snow and made a snowball. We rolled it frontwards and backwards and sideways until it was big and round.

"This will be the snowman's legs," I said.

"Next the tummy," said Bitty Baby.

We rolled and rolled another big snowball. Frontwards and backwards and sideways.

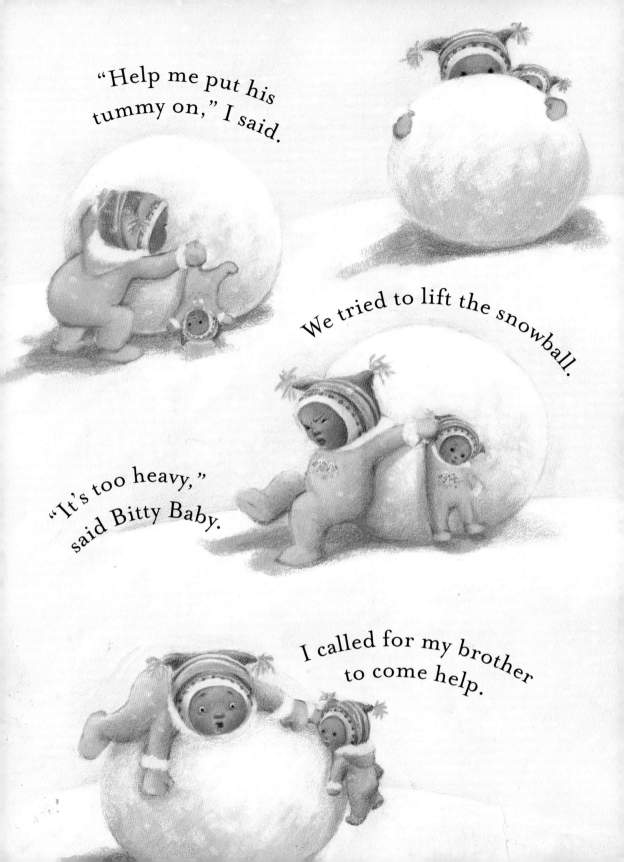

"Help me put his tummy on," I said.

We tried to lift the snowball.

"It's too heavy," said Bitty Baby.

I called for my brother to come help.

"I'm sledding," he called back. "Do it yourself."

Bitty Baby and I looked at each other. "Can't he see that we can't do it ourselves?" she asked.

"Maybe he'll be done sledding soon," I said.

But every time my brother zipped down the hill, he turned right around and climbed back up.

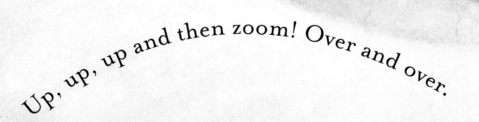

Up, up, up and then zoom! Over and over.

"That does look like fun," I said.

"It looks fun and fast," said Bitty Baby. "And he doesn't need to wait for anyone to help him."

"When I'm big, like my brother, I'll be able to do lots of things," I said. "Even build a snowman."

"*Brrr!* I'm cold," said Bitty Baby. "And I'm tired of waiting."

"I'll tell you a story while we wait," I said. "Then it won't seem so long." We snuggled under a tree.

One snowy day, Bitty Baby met a friendly polar bear.

"I've been waiting and waiting for someone to play with," said Polar Bear. "How about a game of Hide-and-Seek?"

"Okay," said Bitty Baby.

"You hide first," said Bear. He counted to ten.

"Ready or not, here I come!" He spotted Bitty Baby right away. "Now it's my turn to hide."

Bitty Baby counted to ten. "Ready or not, here I come!" she said.

She looked behind and under and up and down. She could not find Bear anywhere. Finally, she called out, "Bear, where are you?"

Polar Bear popped out
of his hiding place. "I'm
good at finding and hiding."
He laughed. "Now let's play
Chase. Try to catch me!"

But Bear zoomed so fast over the ice that
Bitty Baby couldn't catch him.

"How about another game?" asked Bear.

"I know," said Bitty Baby. "Follow the Leader." She skipped across the snow. "I'll be the leader— follow me!"

Polar Bear tried to skip, but his legs got tangled.

"Tippy-toe twirls," said
Bitty Baby. She twirled
around and around.

Polar Bear tippy-toed, but when
he tried to twirl, he landed—
smack—on his bottom.

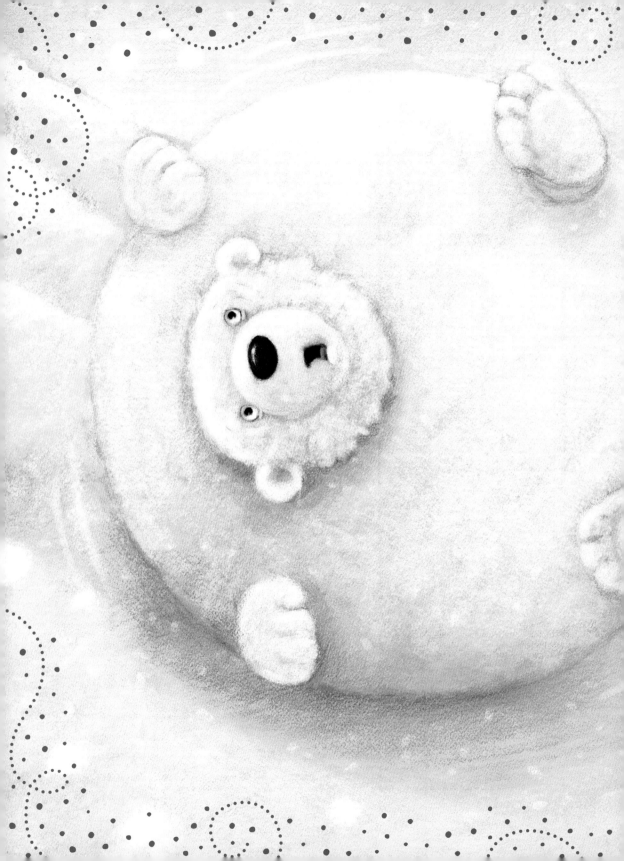

"Here's an easy one,"
said Bitty Baby. She did
a perfect somersault.

"I can do that!" said Bear.
He tucked his head and
began to roll...

and roll...

and roll...

...into a great ball of bear!

Bitty Baby helped brush off the snow.

"I guess I can't twirl and tumble," said Bear.

"And I can't hide and seek in the snow,"
said Bitty Baby.

"Well," said Polar Bear, "if you can't do one thing, do something else!"

And Bitty Baby and Polar Bear made snow angels until it was time to go in for hot cocoa.

The end.

"Polar Bear was smart," said Bitty Baby. "He thought of something they both could do."

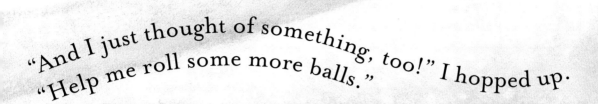

"And I just thought of something, too!" I hopped up.
"Help me roll some more balls."

Bitty Baby and I made five fat snowballs.
We lined them up, one after the other. Then
we found some twigs. "Good job," I said.

"And we did it all by
ourselves," said Bitty Baby.

My brother ran over. "I've never seen a snow caterpillar before," he said. "I'm going to build a snow animal, too!"

While my brother worked on his snow turtle, Bitty Baby and I took a turn on the sled. We zoomed down the hill very, very fast.

As fast as a polar bear.

Maybe faster!

For Parents

Child's Play

Play is the natural language of children. It exercises a child's body and imagination, and it provides a safe place to express feelings and work out conflicts. Through play, your daughter can create her own world and even her own friends.

Playing Alone

Free and unstructured solo play lets your child practice calling the shots, making up the rules, and coping on her own with challenging situations—things she doesn't often get to do. Learning to entertain herself and solve problems helps her develop self-reliance and confidence in her abilities.

Social Play

Playing with siblings and friends provides not just companionship but also an opportunity to develop essential social skills: sharing, taking turns, negotiating, and compromising. Don't rush to step in at the first sign of dispute or friction between playmates—give them a few minutes to see if they can work it out on their own.

Competitive Play

Playing with others will also provide your child's first experience of competition.

Toddlers are often content to imagine that they are the strongest, fastest, biggest kid in the room. But by age four, kids begin to recognize a need to prove their skills to themselves and others. This competitive spirit is a healthy sign of growing self-awareness as children compare themselves with their peers and decide how they want to fit in. Make sure, though, that your little one doesn't feel she has to excel or win in order to gain your approval.

Kids who realize that they are behind in some physical skills (such as ability to catch a ball or do a somersault) might feel anxious about keeping up with their peers. Reassure your child that people have different abilities and gain new skills at different rates. Remind her about all the things she can do now that she couldn't do last year, and boost her self-esteem by asking her to do something she's good at and can feel proud of.

For more parent tips, visit **americangirl.com/BittyParents**

curious

loving

confident